# LUNCH IS ON YOUR OWN

## The Senior Trip

## Suzanne French-Wilson

PublishAmerica
Baltimore

First printing

ISBN: 1-4137-2319-5
PUBLISHED BY PUBLISHAMERICA, LLLP
www.publishamerica.com
Baltimore

Printed in the United States of America

This, my first book, I lovingly dedicate to my husband who believed in me, Barbara and Glenn Lepley, our dear friends, and to all our fellow travelers on the Senior Trip, without whom there would be no book.

# FOREWORD

Have you ever gone on a tour bus vacation? Wouldn't you expect things to be scheduled, organized, and on time? We did.

Sometime last winter, there was a bus trip to Canada planned by the Senior Center in Fort Atkinson, Wisconsin. It was to take place August 29 through September 6. Travel was to be by deluxe motor coach and the brochure hailed it as the French Canadian Castle Tour featuring two nights at the 5-star Le Manoir Richelieu Casino Hotel. The cost was only $679 per person and included 14 meals (eight breakfasts and six dinners). Also included was an escorted tour of Quebec City, an escorted tour of Montreal including the beautiful Notre Dame Basilica, gaming at the amazing Casino de Montreal, not to mention whale watching on the calm waters of Bay St. Catherine. The trip sounded so good, 72 men and women, mostly women, signed up for it. We seniors do love a bargain. There were so many of us, they found it necessary to add a second bus. What were they thinking?

We were on time only once during our entire trip and that

was the last day. There were too many of us, and too much happened—a blow out on one of the busses, an accident that caused our escort to be thrown into the windshield of the bus, and those awful rest stops. We felt like first graders being herded together for a field trip.

The following is the retelling of our journey. It is definitely a one-sided version as told through the eyes of four people who were there. Our names have been changed to keep from being banned from future trips. When you are old, you will understand. I have changed everybody else's name too—just because I can.

Was there anything good about this trip? Was being behind schedule every day and the fact that everyone's butt was taking on the shape of a bucket seat from so much time spent sitting on the bus enough to ruin it? Will we ever go on a bus trip again? Let me take you along as I retrace our steps and you decide.

# Chapter 1

*Introductions - Who Are These People?*

Hello. Come in. Welcome to my book. I was just about to introduce my husband, Sam Spaulding, and our best friends, Cookie and Garry Glennview. Oh yes, and I am Gracie Spaulding. We're glad you stopped in. This book will make more sense if you know who we are—at least the four of us. As with life itself, with its many focal points, it's impossible to see things from the same perspective as others. This is how we saw it.

Sam, my wonderful husband, is one of a kind. For thirty-seven years he worked in the school system, first as a teacher and then as a high school principal. In all those years he missed exactly two half days of work. That's one whole day in thirty-seven years. He was an old-fashioned disciplinarian who ruled with an iron hand inside a velvet soft glove. He loved the kids and to this day attends high school football, basketball, and volleyball games. Also, he supervises the playground during the lunch hour at our local parochial grade school on the days he doesn't work at the hospital. The hospital job he started after he retired and has been working there two days a week for the past 15 years as an outside courier.

Sam was retired when I met him. I remember a time, shortly after we were married. Sam and I had gone out for dinner to a nice restaurant near our retirement home in Winter Haven, Florida. When we walked in the door of the restaurant, we saw several young people all dressed to the nines for prom night. Sam got kind of sentimental and began telling me "school stories" from prom nights past when he had attended the prom as a chaperone. On a whim, he excused himself and went over to the table where the seven young men and women were eating. He just had to talk to them and find out what school they attended, what their plans were after graduation, where the post prom was going to be held, and why there were seven of them, (four girls and three boys) and not eight. Apparently one of the boys had to work right up to the last minute and was going to meet his date at the dance. When he returned to our table, Sam said, "Wouldn't it be fun to pick up the tab for their dinner?"

Since we were newlyweds, I guess he felt he shouldn't do anything like that without discussing it first. I told him if that's what he wanted to do, then he should do it.

He called the waiter over, told him he would like to pay the bill for the prom goers and indicated which table he meant. Sam requested that the waiter ask the young people if they would object. As expected, it was okay with them. I wish you had been there. Those kids were so nice. After dinner, they all came over to our table to thank us personally and they seemed genuinely grateful for the gift. After they had left the restaurant, one boy came back in to thank us again and he added, "I knew I had enough money for the prom but I wasn't sure about the post prom because dinner was a little more than I counted on. Now I don't have to worry. Thank you so much, Mr. Spaulding. I never knew a principal could be that nice." Later the next day one of our friends heard the incident being discussed on talk radio. He mentioned it, not knowing they were discussing us. We never told either.

That's my Sam. He's as organized as he is kind, my Sam is. He chaperoned seventeen-year-olds on senior class trips to New York City and Washington, DC for many years. When it comes to counting noses, no one is better. When he was married to his first wife, he organized a twenty-fifth wedding anniversary party to surprise her. It lasted an entire weekend and included everyone in their wedding party. He managed to get them all together after 25 years and managed to keep the secret from her as well. She was dumbfounded to see so many people she hadn't seen in so many years. At that time, she was battling cancer and the party did much to lift her spirits. Just two years later, she passed away of breast cancer.

Sam would buy me almost anything I really wanted, but he is very frugal when it comes to himself. He clips coupons, shops for bargains, and would always bend down to pick up a penny on the ground. Once he bought a bunch of silent light switches because they were on sale. All of our switches he changed to silent switches. Sam is almost deaf. He wears hearing aids in both ears. Now, how much noise can a light switch make? He got a hell of a deal on them though.

Sometimes he looks like nobody loves him and his mother dresses him funny, but when he gets dressed up, WOW! He has a sense of humor and he loves to tease but he can take a joke too. He served in the Navy during WWII, and that allowed him to go to college on the GI bill. He's quite a guy. So now you know my Sam.

What can I say about Garry? His wife, Cookie, and I often joke that we are married to the same man because Garry and Sam are alike in so many ways. Garry was a high school principal too, and he and Sam shared many of the same philosophies. They worked in neighboring communities and saw each other professionally while they were working, getting together at meetings and conventions. Following retirement, they made time to socialize since Cookie and I got along so well. It's rare to find four people who are all compatible. It's a gift!

Garry is a worker. He would never pay someone to do a job when he can do it himself. He still cuts and splits wood, cuts grass, top-dresses his driveway, paints his house, etc. Not only does he cut grass at his home but he mows the lawn at their cottage near Devils Lake, not far from Madison. Also, he tends to his own personal getaway, sixty acres he bought in the Kickapoo Valley in scenic southern Wisconsin where he was raised. We refer to him as the *Lawn Ranger*. Garry has been an active, (very active) member of the Lions Club for years. It's been over thirty years and he's never missed a meeting when he was in town. I think he is convinced that their annual chicken and corn feed could not survive without him. That may be true but I hope I never have to find out. He tends to the concession stand at Ralph

Park, our local recreational area where all the city leagues play their games. He makes sure that the place is always clean and properly cared for. There is no job beneath him.

The Glennviews and the Spauldings went to Disney World on a joint vacation a few years back. Cookie and I were walking behind Sam and Garry on a hot day in Florida and I couldn't help but laugh. As they walked down the streets of Disney World, they would bend down and pick up litter and carry it until they came to a receptacle where they deposited it. They didn't even know they were doing it. They were talking the whole time and they never missed a word of their conversation. The world is a better place because they are in it.

One thing about Garry, though, he doesn't like to be wrong and sometimes he thinks he knows everything. On a trip we took to the Badlands of South Dakota, we drove. Garry and Sam took turns but I think Garry did most of the driving because he is convinced that he is the better driver. But that's a whole 'nother thing. Gazing out the car windows, Garry and Sam were debating as to what was growing in the fields along the highways. It didn't look like anything that they had ever seen in Wisconsin. This was one I knew! On a trip west I had made before I had met Sam, I was puzzled about the same thing. I stopped by the side of the road, pulled up a stalk of the grain still growing at the side of a harvested field, and when I got to the next stop, asked a local filling station attendant what it was. "Milo," he said. When I told Garry what it was he said, he didn't think that was right. I told him how I knew but I'm sure he couldn't accept the fact that I would know something that he didn't. He kept insisting that it must be sorghum.

Later, we stopped at Mitchell, South Dakota at the Corn Palace, went in and marveled at the decorations. They had covered the walls of the Corn Palace with grain, making some of the most beautiful pictures. Garry saw a man standing down by the stage and we watched from the back as he approached the man, pointed up to a grain picture, and inquired of what it was made. Then he clenched both fists and pounded the air and you could see he was saying, "Damn, she's right!" I have never let him forget that and to this day all I have to do is say "milo" and he cringes.

Garry is a handsome man, six-foot-two-inches tall and still has enough hair to cover most of the top of his head. He is my friend and I will always love him but I can't help but annoy him every chance I get.

Now I would like you to meet my best friend and Garry's wife, Cookie. Cookie is the grand lady of the kitchen. She lives for her family and friends and always has fresh baked goods if you pop in to see her.

Cookie was one of the first people I met after I started dating Sam. When their daughter got married, Sam took me to the wedding. He introduced me to the parents of the bride and they were such a handsome couple. Cookie was beautiful. She looked like a rich lady, very social indeed. She was soft spoken and kind and what I took to be a grand social presence was simply her inner beauty showing through. I would never have figured her for a coffee klatch kind of friend. How wrong I was. She just cleans up nice. There is nothing she can't do. She bakes almost every day. She still hangs her wash out on the line. She sews doll clothes for her granddaughters, works in her garden, does rosemauling, visits the sick, and takes in strangers. She made hand painted stripes on her kitchen wall, she quilts, and makes toilet seat and tank covers for every holiday. Is there anything she can't do? I don't think so.

She is very quiet in her demeanor but if she gets the giggles, she just can't stop laughing. When we travel, Cookie is always in charge of food. She has a kit that she carries with her on trips and when Garry wants coffee, she takes her towel out and lays it across her lap, takes the thermos and pours his coffee and hands it to him. Then she leaves the thermos out in case he wants more. What really drives me crazy is that Garry doesn't see anything unusual in this. Along with coffee she offers him homemade banana bread, chocolate chip cookies, or gorp, a mixture of nuts, chocolate chips, M & M's, raisins, sunflower seeds, and dried fruits. She makes jelly from the cherries on their tree and the grapes that grow in the yard. She buys bushels of apples every year and makes homemade applesauce by the freezer full. She picks strawberries for shortcake and jam. She tends a garden and irons his shirts. HELLO! Cookie, did you know that women have been liberated? I know—you like to do it.

Sam, Cookie, Garry and I get together as often as we can to play a domino game called Spinner. When we first started playing Spinner, we played for a penny a point, but sometimes it seemed like the same people always won. A person could lose over a dollar a game. Then Sam came up with the idea of paying all of our losses into a little tin bank. Besides the losses, we would put in fifty cents per person per get-together. Usually we play two games of Spinner in an evening. It takes us about an hour to play a game but sometimes the conversation gets heated and it takes a lot longer to play. Spinner is a game of dominos with wild spinners on the ends of some of the tiles. We enjoy the game so much we organized it. Here's how.

The host family has the Spinner bank and score sheets. They set the time for the game. I made customized computerized score sheets when we got serious. They are hole-punched and kept in a binder in chronological order of games played. When filled out, they list where we played, who won, who lost, how much was put in the bank, what time we played, and any other information that anyone considers important. The game moves from their house to our house and back. The rules of entertaining are simple. You don't have to clean your house. You don't have to make anything to eat although we have evolved into a ritual of playing one game and then having snacks for the second game. It is never anything elaborate. We make microwave popcorn, or put out a dish of nuts or pretzels. Cookie puts out cookies but I don't. Garry usually has a beer, Sam drinks orange pop or Mountain Dew, and Cookie and I have water. Each couple puts a dollar in the tin bank before we start. There are one winner and three losers, as a rule, for each game. The three losers put their money into the bank. After the games, the visiting couple takes the bank and the score sheets home with them and they know that they are hosts next time. We try to play at least once a week. Twenty-five games in eleven days is the record for number of games played in a given time. We did that when they visited us in Florida one winter. We never get tired of playing Spinner. What happens to all that money? We vote on how to spend it as a group. So far we have gone to the Fireside Dinner Theater here in Fort Atkinson, Sea World in Florida, and spent an overnight at Ho Chunk Casino in Baraboo, Wisconsin. On a trip to Las Vegas, we each took fifty dollars to gamble with. Right now, we have over two hundred dollars in the bank and we're looking for a way to spend it. We're doing all right. Sam keeps track of Spinner statistics and over a time span of several years, everything is about even. The only lopsided thing is you get better snacks at the Glennview's, thanks to Cookie.

What can I say about myself? I'm the only one who never went to college. Well, not until I was fifty-eight years old. That's when I went to Blackhawk Technical College in Janesville, Wisconsin. Computers, that's what I was going to study, but I knew less than nothing about computers and even though I tried my darndest, I couldn't handle it. I switched my courses to a medical office focus and now I am a part-time office assistant in a physical therapy clinic. Maybe I didn't have much formal education, but hey, I'm the one who's writing the book.

Another of my hobbies is making greeting cards. We haven't bought a card since about 1997 because I make them all. The hardest to make are the sympathy cards but I think they are the most appreciated. Conceivably, one could call me a Jack of all trades. I cut my grandchildren's hair as well as Sam's and I have had two holes in one. I took up golf when Sam and I got married. He had played golf his whole life so I took some lessons so I wouldn't embarrass him when we played. My first hole-in-one occurred during couples golf one winter down in Florida. With two other couples watching, I addressed my ball, whacked it a good one with my nine iron, the ball arched way up in the air and landed soft on the green, took one little bounce and rolled into the cup. My "high" lasted for a good three days and I won $112. Sam finally got a hole-in-one of his own. He got his during men's league so he got to be a hero too. Then one day when Cookie and Garry were visiting us in Florida, I challenged Garry to nine holes of golf. Cookie doesn't play and Sam had already played 18 holes that day in the men's league and, according to club rules, couldn't play any more that day. So Garry and I headed for the golf course. We were about even up for the first four holes and then came the tricky fifth. It was a short hole but it was over water. There was a crocodile lying on the edge of the water and a stone wall protecting the green on the far side of the pond. Garry teed off first and put one on the green. It was a sweet shot. But now, the pressure was on me. I addressed my ball, took a nice easy swing and the ball arched beautifully over the water and landed soft on the green. It bounced twice and began to roll toward the pin. It rolled and rolled and then— right before our eyes—it leaned over the lip of the cup and fell in. A hole-in-one! Garry still thinks I cheated somehow but he just can't figure out how. Now it's Sam's turn again. No pressure there, huh?

But let's get back to me. This is hard. I guess you know

I'm writing a book. It seems I like attempting the impossible. My dad always told me that the difficult things in life you should do right away because the impossible ones take longer. If I just keep on typing, pretty soon I'll have a book. There is no reason for me to believe that I could possibly be an author but if I act like one, who knows, it could happen. I just love doing the nearly impossible!

So there you have it. I'm pleased to meet all of you and glad you could drop in to my book. Now that you know us better, our tour bus vacation trip will make more sense. Come along now, get in line, the tour is about to begin.

# Chapter 2

## *Day 1—Hurry Up and Wait*

Sam, Cookie, Garry, and I have enjoyed doing things together ever since Garry and Sam retired fourteen years ago. The four of us got together one evening to play Spinner and the subject of this trip came up. The men liked it because it was cheap. The women liked it because we like to go places together. It sounded like the perfect opportunity to see Canada without any of us having to drive.

When we first signed up, it seemed so far-off—months away. Not knowing how much time we have, (to live, that is) we try not to plan too far ahead. We don't even buy green bananas. We also know that at our age, time flies and if we did sign up, and if we were still alive when the time came to go, we would be happy to be on our way to another adventure. After all, life is what happens to us while we're waiting for our dreams to come true.

August 29 arrived, the dog was in the kennel, and we were ready to go.

Garry, Cookie and their son-in-law, Chad, picked us up at

our house and drove us to the K-Mart parking lot, a minute and a half away. We looked forward to the trip, in part because the contractors were at our house ripping out the bathroom to replace the fixtures, redo walls, and put in a new bathroom floor and replace the floor in the kitchen. It was a good time for us not to be at home. Garry and Cookie didn't mind leaving their house either. Their daughter, son-in-law, two grandchildren, and three cats were living with them while their new house was being built near Milwaukee. They were moving from Indiana to Wisconsin so Mom and Dad's house was the perfect stopping-off place to spend their homeless time of about six weeks. Nuff said? But I digress. Chad dropped us off. There were other people waiting; the bus had not yet arrived.

We were scheduled to leave at 7:30 from Fort Atkinson and then we would go to Whitewater to pick up the Whitewater entourage. The busses arrived, we picked up our bags and headed toward them to get a good seat. That would be a seat in the front of the bus so we're first off when a stop is made.

The bus driver, a portly woman in a navy blue uniform sporting a long reddish pony-tail with a dark blue cloth pony-tail holder shot off the bus and started barking orders. "Stand back! Your names will be called." Of course, we did as we were told. She began calling names and those names she called boarded bus #1. Then she barked, "Everyone whose name I did not call, get on bus #2." That was our bus and, again, we did as we were told. The pony-tailed bus driver will from now on be known as "Schultz" because she reminded us of Schultz from *Hogan's Heroes*. For you younger people, *Hogan's Heroes* was a sitcom about a World War II German prison camp and Schultz was the prison guard. It was a comedy. But, again, I digress. Each bus had a driver and an escort. The driver drives the bus and the escort counts noses, passes out candy, answers questions, puts movies in the VCR, and is in charge of games. The escort on bus #1 was Gretchen, a middle-aged woman who seemed to have control issues. Our bus had two escorts, a local couple who was really excited about being on this trip.

Each individual was allowed one large suitcase to be stowed in the hold under the bus and one carry-on. Everything needed for the first night was to be packed in our carry-on because we would not be unloading the baggage from under the bus the first night. Also there was a time issue. We would have to set our watches ahead one hour when we passed from Indiana into Michigan because we would be crossing a time line. That means we lost another hour just by crossing a border.

We got on the bus and found seats not quite halfway back on the right side as you are facing the back of the bus. Garry and Cookie were on the left side across from us but one row nearer the front. We were going to sit right across from them but the TV screen on our side was too low and too far forward and my head kept bumping it so we moved a row further back. The view of the TV was perfect from there and that would be very handy as we got further into the trip.

We had our luggage properly tagged, our birth certificates in our carry-on luggage, and our picture IDs in our wallets. Our first stop was Whitewater, a college town about six miles from Fort Atkinson. The group was waiting and quickly boarded as soon as their luggage was properly tagged and stowed. Things were looking good.

Our bus driver, also in a navy blue uniform, was a young man who looked to be about six feet tall and in his late 20s. He had a medium dark complexion and neat short hair and appeared to be quite capable. We'll call him Kurt. Our tour escorts were a couple from Whitewater, Rocky and Darlene. They were active at the Senior Center and were offered the opportunity to come along on this trip as escorts. Rocky looked just like Jesse Ventura, the former governor of Minnesota, except he had no visible teeth, so, of course, we called him Jesse (but not to his face). His wife, Darlene, did not elicit good first impressions. She was mid-50s, short, overweight, wore her stomach muscles about mid-thigh, had short, black, straight, spiked hair that was bleached on the top and a part of it dyed bright red. She laughed at everything, loudly, right into the microphone, and when she did, she sounded like Phyllis Diller. Ergo, we named her Phyllis. (But not to her face.)

When I think back, I realize how self-righteous and judgmental we were. Jesse and Phyllis were two of the most honest, loving, and kind people we may ever have the privilege of knowing. They were doing a job that they had never done before and they were doing it valiantly with very little instruction. I'm proud to know them. (My sincere apologies to you both.) But again, I digress.

Everyone was on board now, getting settled in. Phyllis asked to see our IDs. Sam got our bag down from the overhead compartment and produced his birth certificate.

Phyllis took our word that we had a picture ID. Everything was stowed again and we settled into our seats for the long trip. But wait—now they need our medical information. Sam got the bag down again and got what they needed in case of emergency. He re-stowed the bag and settled in once more. We were leaving at last, or so we thought. We were headed out of the parking lot when Phyllis noticed untagged cars in the lot. If one leaves a car in the parking lot without permission of the park authorities, it will be ticketed. So we backed up, Phyllis issued tags, we waited while three people got off the bus, tagged their cars and re-boarded. At last, we were on our way. Kurt was not familiar with Whitewater and was following Schultz but Schultz got lost. She must have gotten her directions from an old version of *Road Maps*. Soooo, an unscheduled tour of Whitewater ensued before we finally got to the highway. At last, our trip was underway and it was only 9:30. Next stop—lunch!

We were not far into the trip when I needed to use the facilities on board the bus. Have you ever done that? That, my friends, is no easy task especially for senior citizens. I was sitting by the window so I had to ask Sam to let me out. He stepped into the aisle and a tad toward the front so I could bend my way out of my seat and into the aisle. As I headed toward the back of the bus, I held on tightly to the backs of the seats trying not to touch anyone's hair. When I reached the back of the bus, I opened the door, stepped in, pulled the door shut and immediately sat down hard on the seat. Fortunately, the cover seat was down so I didn't fall in. That move wasn't planned, it just happened. I grabbed for the grab bar and tried to stand up. I was sure we were taking a shortcut through a freshly plowed field. The bus was moving fast and it felt like there were no shock absorbers 'cause I was bouncing around in there like popcorn in a pan. Sitting was the easy part; gravity took care of that. I guess if you gotta go, you gotta go. I was glad I had an air sanitizer spray. There was no water because that would be unsanitary. Fortunately, I packed some hand sanitizers, lotion, Band-Aids, antibiotic cream, and hair spray. I never needed the hair spray.

Game time! It was 10:00 and the name of the game was "Guess the Product." Phyllis gave us a slogan and we had to guess the product to which it referred. After that she played "Interesting Facts." That was simply a list of useless facts that she read to us and we wondered why. For game #3 we needed to fill out forms with personal information. Then she called on each one to state their name and tell a little bit about himself or herself to the group. That one was the biggest flop of all. We were beginning to wonder exactly what we had gotten ourselves into, when Phyllis announced that we were going to make a pit stop soon. Then they passed a basket of hard candy and we helped ourselves to lifesavers and mints. Actually, I passed because I couldn't stop wondering exactly how clean my hands were.

Can you imagine the Burger King for a pit stop? We had ten minutes. If they had only one bathroom and there were two stalls, how long would it take two busloads of people to get relief? Never mind, that was a rhetorical question. Next stop: lunch in Chesterfield, Indiana.

Aside: If Sam were driving in his car, we would have left home at 4:30 in the morning and would probably be close to the Canadian border by now, even with a stop for breakfast.

11:00 a.m.: It was "get acquainted" time. Phyllis called on each one to state their name, hobbies, and what they wanted to get out of the trip. When called on, I said I like to sleep, eat, travel, and play Spinner. She never questioned what Spinner was and she never called on Sam. Maybe she prejudged him. He surely didn't look like the nice guy he really is. Disorganization makes him snarly and on this trip, if he were a dog, one would worry that he might bite.

The bus driver exited the highway and pulled into an area where there were several fast food places. We had our choice of various eateries since lunch was on our own. We hauled ourselves out of our seats and tried to walk. It felt like there was a hot poker in each hip and my knees didn't want to lock into place to keep me from falling flat on my face. Eventually everything was working okay and I could walk once again. Garry, Cookie, Sam and I chose Taco Bell because it was the farthest away from the bus and would give us some much needed exercise. After lunch we walked a little more before re-boarding. Once we were moving, Jesse popped a movie into the VCR and voila, the movie was flashing on all eight TV screens. We watched John Candy and Dan Aykroid in a summer vacation flick, "The Great Outdoors" and time passed rather quickly.

Shortly after 5:00, we made another pit stop. It was only

the first day and I could hardly stand up. How was I going to feel by the time I got to Canada?

After driving another hour and a half, we stopped at the Fire Mountain Restaurant in Lansing, Michigan for supper. It was the first of many buffets to come and it was enormous. A waitress seated us in a private dining room that was a tad overcrowded, but then there were 72 of us. It was nice that we could all be seated in one room. One would think we were children home from school at the end of the school day after skipping lunch. We ate just about everything that didn't move. The only difference between school children and us was that we ate slower. When we finished, we were once again lined up outside the door of the necessary room.

The bus drivers ate and then left to fill the busses with gas and wash the bugs off the windshields. It took them longer than they anticipated as they didn't return to the restaurant until 8:15 p.m. to pick us all up. We were late leaving and had a long way to go. After re-boarding, it was time for another movie, "Catch Me If You Can" with Tom Hanks and Leonardo di Caprio. I had seen it in the theater but it was worth another look. If nothing else, it made the time pass more quickly.

At 11:00, we arrived at the Duty Free Shop on the American side of the St. Lawrence River just before we got into Canada. Both busses poured all their passengers into that store at once. The bathroom facilities were acceptable; it was a welcome stop. Jesse and Phyllis suggested that we exchange about $20 American money for Canadian currency so that's what we did. Everyone was happy because we got $26.60 Canadian back. I bought a bottle of water for $.69 American. It was a worthwhile stop but after we got back on the bus we still had to go through the dreaded customs. We were told to stay quiet, answer questions only if we were asked, and don't joke about anything. I don't think anyone was in a joking mood at that point, but you never know. A customs agent boarded the bus, looked around, said something to the driver, indicated we were okay, and gave us the thumbs up to enter Canada. We all breathed a sigh of relief because we were all tired and we just wanted to be on our way and get to our motel.

Eventually, somewhere between midnight and 1:30 a.m. we got to London, Ontario and our motel. We grabbed our carry on bags, found our rooms and went to bed. I'm not sure about the exact time line because I fell asleep on the bus. Sam and I can't agree on the time and you know how old people are. Anyhow—sleep at last!

# Chapter 3

## *Day 2—Are We There Yet?*

The alarm was set for 7:00 a.m. When it went off we were still sleepy-eyed and a tad on the crotchety side, but we got up, showered, shampooed, threw everything in our overnight bags and went to breakfast.

The motel offered a simple but tasty Continental breakfast of bagels, bananas, cereal, juice, and coffee. All of us went to the dining area about the same time and I pitied the poor travelers who came for breakfast and found 72 seniors taking up every corner of space in the dining area. We don't give an inch when it comes to eating. We ate our bagels, juice, and coffee, gathered our belongings, used the bathroom one last time, and headed for the bus. Getting back on that bus was not our first choice for what we wanted to do but we did it anyway at exactly 9:00 a.m. All of us, that is, except one couple. They must have heard 9:15. We waited for them and after all the noses were counted for the third time, we finally got under way.

Like yesterday, we started day 2 with a game. Our first

game was one I like to call the *information game*, remember, like the one we played the day before. How fun! Not! The next game was a *"finish the saying"* game and I won! Phyllis sent Jesse down the aisle with a *Little Debbie Cream Pie*. It eventually crumbled in my carry-on bag and I threw it out. Cookie won a cookie too. Cookie has probably baked homemade cookies every day of her life but I'll bet she never made any with preservatives. I wonder whether she ever ate her free cookie.

So far, this trip has not been much fun. Sam and Garry could have shaved at least 2 ½ hours off our time if they had been in charge. I'm sure glad they weren't. There wouldn't have been any games. We need to get into the spirit of this trip. We need to catch up on our sleep. We need to not drink too much so we don't have to use the facilities on the bus. That little room is getting rank. In fact, it makes the back of the bus a tad stinky. Okay, it smells like an outhouse.

At 11:00, we made a pit stop. So far we have not had much fun unless, of course, one really likes to watch pine trees and semis go by. We did pass some decorated lawn animals (mostly cows). Phyllis decided they were moose. She also informed us that Oshawa, Ontario was the last place to get a milk shake on this tour. I don't know whether or not anyone put that to the test. We didn't.

Meals were never missed. At 1:00, we stopped at a food mall in the middle of nowhere. There were so many people there, you'd think they were giving away free tickets to see the Glenn Miller orchestra. It was more crowded than a pre-Christmas 50% off sale at Toy's "R" Us. Adding 72 more people who were all in a hurry was ludicrous. But, that's what we did. It was the only show in town.

🚌 🚌

The four of us had a plan. Sam and Garry stood in line at a sub shop to get sandwiches "to go" while Cookie and I stood in line to get into the bathroom. While we were standing in line, we met a woman from Toronto who was on her way home from vacationing in Quebec. She was with her mother who was also very nice. (That's what we do when we're in line—we talk to people.) Then our turn came to use the facilities so I really don't know any more about the nice Canadians. When we finally met up with the men, they had gotten our lunch and were waiting patiently for us to join them. We sat on the curb next to the bus and ate our sandwiches, took some pictures, and got back on the bus. Just a few more hours and we should be somewhere.

It was movie time again! This time we watched "Snow Dogs" with Cuba Gooding, Jr. I got a nap in too—mostly during the movie.

Earlier today while we were cruising down the highway, we saw, on the other side of the road, what was left of what had been a really bad accident. There was the burnt out shell of one car lying in the ditch and a couple more that were badly crashed in. It looked like a semi and two or three cars were involved and we knew not everyone could have gotten out alive. I offered a quick silent prayer for all involved as well as for their families. Traffic was backed up for miles in the opposite direction. It must have been difficult for the ambulances to get through. So far, I hate this trip.

It was 5:15 and we were stopped but I don't know where we were. We were told to stay on the bus while Phyllis went to the other bus to speak with Gretchen. Phyllis came back and explained that we had about an hour to go before we got to our motel. I don't know why she had to go to the other bus to find that out. They were in constant radio contact the whole trip.

At approximately 6:10 p.m., we pulled up to the Comfort Inn at Laval (Montreal), Quebec. This night we got our big suitcases. There was no rush as far as eating was concerned because we didn't have to get back on the bus until morning. But for right then, we had to remain on the bus until someone from the motel came out to the bus and distributed room keys, dinner coupons, etc. The sun was setting, the weather was cool, the other bus had unloaded, and we were trying to be patient. Finally, at 6:45, it was our turn to get off the bus. After getting our keys, we learned that we were on the second floor and there was no elevator. Sam has a heart condition and shouldn't be hauling heavy luggage up a flight of stairs. We got into a heated argument about his fragile condition and I was ready to kill him if he lived through the ordeal. He not only hauled our luggage, he helped a lady who had a cane with her luggage.

We should have been eating supper by 7:15. Well, that didn't happen. While sitting in the dining room munching on rolls and drinking water, we were discussing how slow the service was and how hungry we were. It was 8:45 before we were served and by then we were getting a little grumpy. We made the best of it, though, because, finally, we were eating and food really does soothe the savage beast. Or is that music? I forget. After dinner, we returned to our rooms and our big suitcases. It was 9:30 and Sam was exhausted. Immediately he undressed and went to bed. I, on the other hand, have my nighttime ritual I must tend to. Every night it's the same thing. After washing my face and brushing my teeth, I take my medication and I get my clothes ready for the next day.

Moving around freely was such a treat after being confined to a bus seat all day. I didn't mind that Sam had unplugged right away. I needed that time for myself to unwind a little before turning in. My big suitcase was on the luggage stand where I could get at it easily. I tried to open it but it was locked. That wasn't possible. I never locked my suitcase. But it was locked. Sam! Sam must have locked my suitcase. 'Why would he do that?' I wondered. He was already asleep and now I had to wake him up and yell at him. I had to yell because he had removed both of his hearing aids. Getting back to sleep was never a problem for Sam though, so I shook him a little.

"Sam? Did you lock my suitcase?" I asked.

"Yes," he said.

"Why?" I asked.

"Because it had keys," he said.

"I need the key. Where is it?"

"It's in my billfold," he said, and turned over.

He always leaves his wallet lying on the dresser. I found

it, opened it, and searched. I looked in every corner of that wallet and there were no keys. Well would you look at that! There was a hole in Sam's wallet and the keys were gone. By then, I was over-tired, frustrated, and just plain mad. I woke up Sam a second time.

"There's a hole in your wallet and the keys are gone."

"They can't be," he said in that "I'll show you" voice and he got up and stumbled over to the table where his wallet lay so that he could prove to me that the keys were there.

Whaddaya know—no keys.

I wanted to ask what he was going to do next but I didn't dare. He needed some kind of a tool so he could open the lock. I found a paper clip in the desk drawer and gave it to him. He tried the old "bend the paper clip into a luggage-opening device" trick. That didn't work. He seemed upset that I didn't carry pliers in my purse. I would have told him what to do with pliers if he ever found any but we weren't speaking at that point. Besides, he didn't have his hearing aids in and I would have had to yell. That would not have been good. The next thing I knew he was putting on his pants and shoes and out he went into the night in search of something he could use to bend the paper clip into a shape that would work. By 10:00 or so he was back with a pair of pliers. The restaurant manager, Rock, had some in the trunk of his car. He loaned them to Sam to be returned the next morning. Sam came back to the room, bent the paper clip, opened the lock and stretched out his hand, palm up, toward my suitcase as if to imply, "There is your precious suitcase," and went back to bed, all without saying a word. In 3 ½ minutes, he was snoring again.

I finished my ritual, stewing the while, then climbed into bed. I thought, *I'll never be able to go to sleep now. Every nerve in my body is on red alert. How can he do that, go to sleep so fast? He can just climb into bed and go right back to sleep before his head makes a dent in the pillow. It'll take me forever. I guess I'm just supposed to close my eyes and the magic sleep ferry comes and touches me with her magic wand and, presto, I'm asleep. Yeah, like that's going to happen. I could try to read for awhile but I know the light wouldn't bother him. Even if I made noise, he'd never know it because he doesn't have his hearing aids in. I just wish I could fall asleep. Umm zzzzzz.*

# Chapter 4

## *Day 3—Sightseeing, Gambling, Eating*

Boy, did I sleep! You'd have thought it was sex or drugs that made sleeping that gratifying but I'm pretty sure it was just the fact that we had our big suitcases. F.Y.I., Sam returned the pliers to Rock.

Breakfast was at 8:00. We enjoyed a tasty breakfast of eggs, bacon, sausage, potatoes, croissants, and coffee. There was plenty of time to get ready to leave by 9:30 for a bus tour of Montreal.

This time we had a French tour guide on board, Louis (pronounced Loo ee'). Everyone was in a good mood and we were on time and on our way. After riding just a short distance, Kurt made a right turn into what proved to be the entrance to the beautiful L'Oratoire St. Joseph. Everyone got off the bus at the grand statue of St. Joseph and we crossed the street carefully because there was a steady stream of cars occupied by people on their way to Mass. Once we were across the street, we gathered around Louis at the statue's base. From there we could see clearly the

Oratory and all the steps ascending to this monumental place of worship. There were people climbing the steps on their knees, saying a prayer at each step. We listened to Louis crank off all the pertinent facts about the Oratory. There was not enough time to climb the steps, let alone go into the L'Oratorie St. Joseph. We crossed the street again, back to the bus, boarded, and from the windows of the bus saw the Notre Dame Basilica, high on a hill not far from the Oratory.

Next stop was The Underground City of Montreal where we were to have lunch. The Underground City is a huge mall located beneath a big Protestant church in downtown Montreal. It had a very large food court at the center (the mall, not the church). Of course, lunch was on our own.

How perfect! A food court was an excellent place for 72 people to have their lunch and find acceptable bathroom facilities. After de-bussing, we walked a short distance and entered a glass-enclosed area accessible from the busy street. There were escalators running up and down from the busyness of the street above to the quiet atmosphere of the mall below. Those with canes could navigate the escalators with care but a woman in a wheelchair had to find a place to eat on the street level. All the rest of us went underground. We ate and shopped, and looked at as much as we could in the little time that we had. Then, after another stop at the restroom, we headed toward the up escalator and back to the street. As I left the restroom, a woman informed me that I had a long ribbon of toilet paper stuck to my shoe. I thought that only happened in the movies. Finally, we headed back up the escalators to the bustling street. It was a great place to "people watch." It was a good thing, too, because the bus was late.

The bus didn't show up until about 1:20. I don't know why; I never heard any explanation. All I know is that it wasn't our fault. Yes, I *would* like a little cheese with my whine.

Montreal, the word, is a blending of Mount and Royale. That's just a little bit of trivia I thought you'd like to know.

Our guide, Louis, was great. He had a heavy French accent but he spoke slowly enough so that everyone could understand him. He pointed out many things about Montreal that we might have missed if he had not been with us. We toured Montreal and saw what Louis wanted us to see by looking out the bus windows. There were row houses, each with a flight of outside stairs going from street level up two and sometimes three stories. The buildings were quaint and the city was crowded and I couldn't help but wonder how all those steps were managed when the snow started to fall. It was the only way into those houses and Montreal gets about 50 feet of snow each winter, according to Louis. There were sidewalk cafes and everyone spoke French. All of the signs were in French and we began trying to translate signs and pronounce French words. I wish we could have gotten closer to the people and their culture. There was so much to see and we barely scratched the surface.

Parlay voo fran say? Neither do I.

We toured more of the city after lunch and then went to Olympic Park in Montreal. The brochure stated that we would enjoy a cable car ride up the Montreal Tower. I expected individual cars strung by heavy cables on a pulley climbing all the way to the top of a tall building. In each car, there would be two to four people oohing and aahing all the way to the top. I thought we would be able to look out over the sides of the cable car and down on the city while our knuckles turned white from holding too tightly to a bar. Instead, we were herded into a very large glass-topped elevator-like structure that sped its way to the top of the tower. The tower was originally designed to operate the domed roof over the Montreal Stadium. It was to be used during the Summer Olympics. However, it was not completed in time and therefore, never completely finished. As a result, it is the only stadium that has a retractable roof that doesn't retract. When we got to the top, there was a panoramic view of the city and a gift shop. We waited for an empty cable car to come for us so we could go down again. All of us had to travel down together. I think they did not trust us to go down by ourselves and wait for the others. When we tried it, we were stopped in our tracks.

At this point our guide left us and we departed for the Casino de Montreal where we would eat dinner at an elegant buffet and then gamble if we wanted to. I love to eat and I love to gamble, so I was really pumped for this part of the trip.

Our two busses pulled up to the back door of the Casino de Montreal and we waited patiently, as instructed. Eventually a Casino representative showed up, boarded our bus, and issued meal vouchers and match play tickets. As soon as we entered the Casino, we were to go to the Cashier and trade our match play ticket in for $10 (Canadian money). We could keep it, gamble with it, save it for our grandchildren, put it in the collection basket at Church, whatever. I knew they really wanted me to spend it in the Casino so that's what I did.

The Casino was a labyrinth of gambling floors, elevators, circular hallways, gaming tables, and slot machines. There was a cacophonous din that only increased with each quarter I lost. In no time at all I had lost $35 and the thunder in my head made it seem as if it would explode, and I hadn't even had dinner yet. I couldn't afford to keep playing but I wanted to. Did I tell you that I could easily be a gambling addict? Sam was very happy when I decided to stop gambling and find the buffet. After many elevator rides and stopping to ask directions from several people, we finally found it.

What a nice surprise that was. Sam and I were seated at a little out of the way table removed from the noise of the machines and the atmosphere did much to improve my mood. Everything on the buffet looked good and by then we were hungry.

We started with a glass of wine (not included in the price of the dinner.) Then we had a bowl of cream of carrot soup. I didn't care for it but Sam did. I indulged in mussels and clams, rolls, and butter. Then I decided to choose from the pasta bar; the toppings were all made to order and I ordered everything that was available. We had such a pleasant meal and my mood changed from shrew master to serene queen. At the dessert table, there was a fountain of flowing chocolate to enhance fresh fruit or ice cream or cake. I opted for the fruit but not the chocolate. Sam, on the other hand, would put chocolate on cardboard, and eat it if it were available. He was happy as a pig in mud. He had the chocolate … a couple of times. It took a long time for the waitress to bring our bill for the wine but that was okay. We were enjoying the evening. Sam was glad that the meal was included in the price of the trip because the wine was $7 a glass.

After dinner, we walked around for awhile and watched the gamblers gamble. I really wanted to play again but if I had, I wouldn't have had any gambling money left for when we got to the next Casino. Soon it was time for the bus to arrive to take us to our hotel for the night. It had been a long day and I was ready for a good night's sleep. Even a motel bed sounded good.

# Chapter 5

## *Day 4—Luggage, Bingo, Bathrooms, and Shrines*

Bon jour! Monday—it should have been a snap. It started out great! I was in a good mood. I had all of our bags ready the night before because we were to have our luggage ready for pick up by 7:15a.m. We did that. Breakfast was at 7:30. We were there. There was no reason to be late or behind schedule all day. WRONG!

All of the luggage for both buses had not been properly marked and was not being put on the right bus. Before we could go anywhere, the people who boarded the bus in Jefferson had to get off the bus and find their luggage from the entire luggage collection. They did as instructed and then got back on the bus. I thought we were on our way. But no, not yet. All of the Fort Atkinson people had to get off the bus and claim their luggage. We did that, and then got back on the bus. Sam was about ready to blow a fuse. It certainly didn't help things any when I remembered that I had left my sweater in the room and he had to go back into the motel, stop at the desk to get a room key, go back to the room, find my sweater, and return to the bus. I thanked him quietly and then kept my mouth shut for awhile.

Hey! It's time for BINGO. I paid my dollar and won a coupon for a bottle of water that cost $1. I paid a buck. I won a buck. Life is good.

We made an unscheduled tour of Trois Rivieria (Three Rivers.) Actually, Schultz (you remember, the driver of bus #1) made a wrong turn so we got to do some sightseeing. However, without an escort to tell us what sights we were seeing, it seemed more like a detour through a quaint little Christmas village. I bet it was a really neat place. We tried to read the signs and, although our translations from French to English were getting better, we still didn't know for sure what we had seen.

Ahhh, a rest stop at last. This time it was a roadside rest area. We were ready for a break from the tedium of sitting still and looking out the window, so we eagerly got off the bus. The facilities inside for the men were more than adequate. However, there were at least 50 women with full bladders and just 5 inadequate stalls. The line of women standing on one foot and then the other went from the parking lot to the lobby, to the anteroom of the restroom, to the main restroom, to the next available stall. The good news was that the facilities had paper towels as well as electric hand dryers. Paper towels speed things up a lot. The instructions on those electric hand dryers should read, "Push button to start, hold hands under dryer, rub hands together briskly, then wipe hands on pants." Everyone eventually got her turn and we all got back on the bus.

After riding just a short time we arrived at the Shrine of St. Anne de Beaupre. The town was Beaupre. It was St. Anne's Shrine. Everything takes longer to say when you say it in French. But, once again, I digress. I was looking forward to seeing the shrine since St. Anne was Jesus's grandmother; I figured we had a lot in common (being grandmothers and all) and so I wanted to spend some time at her house. First things first though. The plan was that we were to get something to eat (lunch was on our own) and then visit the shrine or the gift shop, or do whatever we wanted. We had approximately 2 ½ hours so Garry, Cookie, Sam, and I decided to find a place to eat that was a little off the beaten path. So, while the rest of the group was standing in line, entering through the exit door of a cafeteria, we were off exploring. We came across a quaint little restaurant in the home of one of the locals. We were warmly welcomed and escorted through the main part of the house, through the kitchen, and out onto the back porch. It was delightful. The proprietors didn't speak a lot of English and we spoke no French but that was never a problem. There were English subtitles on the menu and that helped. I ordered a local beer to start things off. Then I had shepherd's pie with beets and catsup and an espresso. I don't remember what the others had.

It was cool on the porch and it started to rain. By the time our food was served, it was raining hard but coming straight down so we didn't get wet. A man who must have lived in town came up the back steps of the porch and went right to what seemed to be his favorite table. He must have ordered "the usual" because he was served, ate, and was out of there in no time. Meanwhile, we enjoyed being there together. We talked and laughed and tried our French out on each other and our waitress. She took a picture of the four of us at the table and I took one of Sam and our waitress. When we were finished with our lunch, we used their bathroom facilities (just like home) and then left by the front door. Cookie and I had our pictures taken on the little porch out front. The four of us left feeling like we had gotten to know our Northern neighbors a little better.

We were full and glad for the walk to the Shrine. We realized that time was running short; I guess we took too much time at the restaurant. Reaching the shrine, we entered quietly and I felt a holy presence. I believe that St. Anne came to greet us. It seemed as if she were not alone. I could feel the presence of angels as well. There was a welcoming aura that left peace in my heart. I hope I can return there some day. Many had visited there before us as was evidenced by the countless discarded canes and crutches left there by those who had been healed by St. Anne. Grandmothers are so special, aren't they? I realize that this may be difficult for everyone to understand, but it's my story and my faith and I pray for all who read this little book. I ask for a miracle for each one of you.

There was no time left to go to the gift shop. We had to get back on the bus and continue on our way. We were headed for the Charlevoix region of Quebec and the five star Hotel and Casino, Le Manoir Richelieu. The Casino de Charlevoix was on the grounds of the Hotel. We were looking forward to fine dining and then more gambling at the Casino. It was just before dusk when we arrived and we went straight to our rooms. A basket of goodies was on the table by the bed and there were a well-stocked bar and refrigerator. We were warned ahead of time not to eat or drink anything in the room without checking the prices first. A little school lunch size bag of pretzels was $6. Sam really likes to nibble but at those prices, it was not hard for him to leave that stuff alone. It was a good thing supper was included in the price of our trip or he would have gone looking for a Cracker Barrel. By the time we found our room and got somewhat settled in, the sun had set and we really couldn't see much of our surroundings.

We decided to dress for dinner so I put on the only dressy outfit I had with me. It wasn't real fancy but it packed well. How chic can I look with my orthopedic shoes anyway? We looked the best we could and started out to find the proper dining room. It was another buffet. The fare was grand and we enjoyed a leisurely dinner with wine and dessert. There were linens on the tables and linen napkins for our laps. The waiters and waitresses were well dressed in somewhat formal attire. The desserts were French pastries and lots of whipped cream. The service was excellent but it was still a buffet.

As far as the grounds were concerned, Le Manoir Richelieu was definitely a five star hotel. Indoors, all of the public spaces were grand and deserved the five star rating. But the rooms were only three star rooms. They were small to average in size. There were two double beds, a desk, a TV armoire and a bathroom. The only difference between that room and a Ramada room was that the toiletries came in bigger bottles. The prices of the snacks were absurd. I can't imagine that anyone who ate at that buffet would have room for snacks anyway. After dinner we returned to our room to change clothes. Sam put his pajamas on and headed for bed. I put on my comfy clothes and headed for the Casino with Garry and Cookie.

The Casino is a casino. If you play long enough, it will take all your money. We did go to the cashier and picked up our free $10 to gamble with. We were to get $10 the next night too. My luck had changed a little bit. This time I think I about broke even, gambling wise. About 11:00, I decided to go back to our room and go to bed. I don't know what happened to Cookie and Garry. I know Cookie likes to play nickel machines one nickel at a time and there just weren't any of those. They probably went to bed. After all, tomorrow is another day.

# Chapter 6

## *Day 5—Whale Watching*

Everyone on the tour was excited about whale watching. Some who were unable to keep a steady foot opted not to go because they had to be able to climb steps and walk on unsteady surfaces. They were restricted by their physical limitations but their spirits really wanted to go. They just couldn't. For the majority, we were ready to see some whales in their natural habitat.

The day started with a hot breakfast at the hotel. We had plenty of time after breakfast to look around outside to see what everything looked like in the light of day. We walked around the grounds and marveled at how the whole area came to life when the sun came up. There were many outdoor spaces that were breathtaking. The hotel was located on the banks of the St. Lawrence River. It was high on a hill and you could see the river and surrounding area for miles. There were flower gardens in full bloom and green spaces and grassy areas all the way to the sea. The smell of the flowers in the air and the warm sun on your shoulders made you wish that time would stand still, if even for a little while. We learned from some of the others who didn't go to the Casino the night before that there was an outdoor swimming pool that was open year 'round. According to them, it was warm and steamy and swimming and playing in the warm water and cold air enabled the swimmers to sleep like babies. It truly was a beautiful place. For those who didn't want to swim or gamble, there was a bonfire on the hotel grounds where anyone could partake of the sights and smells of a crisp autumn evening by the fire. The fire pit was a rectangular stone framed area with firewood at hand nearby. I understand they even had marshmallows available for anyone who wanted them. It must have been like a little trip back in time to Girl/Boy Scout camp. I wonder if they made s'mores. Remember them?

Before we knew it, it was time to board the bus for our trip to Bay St. Catherine and the boat that would take us to the fjords in the bay, the natural habitat of the whales. It was emphasized that there were no guarantees that we would see any whales. If they showed up, good fortune was ours. If they didn't, the tales of past trips would have to suffice.

Our guide explained that if whales were spotted, someone would yell out the location of the sighting. For example, we were to think of the boat as a clock. The front of the boat was 12:00, the back of the boat was 6:00, the right side was 3:00 and the left side was 9:00. So if someone yelled that there were whales at 11:00 we knew to look toward the front and a little left.

Before long, the sightings started and soon they were often and in all directions. Menke, (pronounced Meen-kee) whales were first to be seen. They were medium sized and dark brownish black and we usually saw only one or two at a time. Beluga whales seemed to be everywhere. They were white and traveled in large groups called pods. Then there were baleen whales, named for the shape of the columns of horny, elastic plates that hang down in fringed, parallel columns from their upper jaw. The baleen serves as a strainer that catches plankton while the whale is feeding. It is not only useful for the whale but baleen was used to make whalebone stays for corsets a really long time ago. Not only do I want to protect the whales, I think whalebone corsets will never make a comeback. You can't breathe in those things. It's kind of like buying a pair of size 16 slacks and wearing the belt for a size 10. Really, breathing is better.

Cookie shared with us her enthusiasm for the perfect fjords that surrounded us. Personally, I couldn't tell the difference between a fjord and a Chevy. But after she explained how the fjords were formed having vertical rock formations sprouting tall trees up and down the walls of solid rock, I had a new admiration for Mother Nature. It was a sight to behold.

After being up on deck for awhile, I began to get cold. If I ever go whale watching again, gloves and a hat will be high on my list of things to take along. Lunch was on our own and we were on a boat that served food so we bought our lunch on board. Coming down into the warm, protected area below from the icy cold air on deck was a welcome relief. The smell of hot soup and steamy coffee began warming us as soon as our nostrils picked up the scents of those comforting aromas. It warmed the cockles of our hearts. Most people stayed in the enclosed area and sat at tables to eat. Some never did go out on deck but chose to watch through the glass surrounding the protected areas. The plates were paper and the flatware was plastic but no one seemed to mind. The warm soup and coffee were most welcome. And we could see whales just by looking out the big windows.

After about 2 ½ hours of whale watching, we returned to shore and once again to the bus. This time our destination was a new restaurant, Le Manoir Charlevoix. It was a comfortable place even though there were more tables set up than there really was room for comfortably. The four of us were seated in an out of the way corner that was far removed from the kitchen. Our area seemed a little quieter than some of the others. At any rate, it was easier to talk and we did have lots to talk about.

After the main course but before dessert, I needed to find a restroom so I excused myself from the table, wound my way through all the diners, found a waiter and asked for directions to the restroom. He turned me around, pointed toward a sign and said in broken English, "Do you see that sign? It says 'Chambers.'" Yes, I did. Following the arrows on the sign, up the stairs I went and down the hall. Dead-end! Retracing my steps, I went as far as I could in the opposite direction. That led to an exit door with a fire escape. Surely he wouldn't have sent me up the stairs inside to go down the stairs outside, so I turned around and went back up the hall. I decided the door I was looking for must have been the door closest to the stairway I came up initially. There didn't seem to be any other solution so I went to the door closest to the top of the stairs. I tried the door and it was unlocked. As I entered, a woman screamed. I almost didn't have to go anymore. Back down the stairs in a flash I went. Finding the waiter, I told him my tale of woe, and he laughed, as did several of the wait staff. He pointed to the sign again. This time he directed my eye a little to the left and it came to rest on a sign that said "TOILETTES." The wait staff was still laughing when I came out. I learned later that "Chambers" are hotel rooms. I'm glad I never saw that woman who screamed.

I returned to the table and ate my dessert without saying another word. After dinner, we boarded our bus for the four-minute trip back to Le Manoir Richelieu. It was our last night there so we decided to gamble a little before we went to bed. This time Sam went with me to the Casino. He handed me $10 so I could start gambling right away while he stood in line for the free money. I found the lucky poker machine that I had played a little the night before and put my free $10 into the machine. Eventually, without putting in any more of my own money, I played all evening and cashed out $167.25. What a day! Wasn't that nice of Sam to stand in line for me so I wouldn't have to? I wish he had won too.

# Chapter 7

## *Day 6—Sightseeing, Flat Tires, &*
## *McDonald's*

We were up, showered, dressed, and off to breakfast by 7:45. This was the day we left the castle and our fairy tale existence. For breakfast we dined on omelettes with onions, peppers, bacon, and cheese. There were bread choices of wheat, white, oat, multi-grain, cranberry, cinnamon, and frosted. There were bread, bagels, and Danish. Among our main choices was cold oatmeal/fruit soup that was quite tasty. Fruits, nuts, juice, coffee, crepes, and cheeses were all offered for our dining pleasure and it was only breakfast. The counters were adorned with lard sculptures that were works of art. Of course, we had to touch one. Why do we do that when we know we shouldn't?

But, alas, time marches on, and soon it was time to board the bus and head for Quebec and a tour of Old Quebec City. We were to meet our tour guide at the Drill Hall across from The Parliament Building, which we did. He boarded our bus and explained the rules of the day. Just in case we didn't know, he explained that lunch would be on our own. There were so many cafes from which to choose we might have a difficult time deciding where to eat. After receiving our instructions, we were dismissed on a large city square about a block away from Grande Allee, the sight of our luncheon choices.

The four of us set out to walk through Grande Allee, several city blocks of sidewalk cafes and little shops. We wanted to see what each place had to offer before we settled for one. Sidewalk cafes were lined up one right after the other on both sides of the street. They displayed their menus curbside so one could decide whether or not it was affordable or if the choices were acceptable. Even Burger King had a sidewalk café. Some ate there. Others opted for pizza places. Others went to places that offered really tall beer glasses filled to the brim with that amber thirst-quenching brew. We checked out most of the restaurants and decided to eat at the first one we had come to. Isn't that always the way?

There was a table for four situated near the center of the dining area and not too far from the street. The hostess seated us there. The temperature was in the 70s but the sun was quite warm so the big colorful umbrella that shaded our table was a welcome addition. We all sat down and studied the menu both in French and in English. It's fun to try reading the French but we had to check our choices in English to make sure we were ordering what we wanted. I ordered mostaccioli with clams, shrimp, and mussels and a local beer. I remember wanting to try everything. It was oh so French. The seafood/pasta choice was a good one. We ate and we talked and laughed and had a wonderful time. Once again, we asked the waitress to take our picture and we were in another world that afternoon. When we had finished eating, Cookie and I needed chocolate. I asked our waitress to bring us something choc-o-lat and four forks. She smiled and said, "Oui," and disappeared. Before we could finish guessing what she would bring, she was back with a BIG slab of heavy, dark, chocolate cake with gooey thick chocolate sauce poured over the top. It was served on a chilled, white plate that was drizzled with raspberry sauce. It was to die for. Don't you just hate salivating in public? Each of us would take a bite and pass the plate. It went round and round until we couldn't eat any more because it was so rich. We left probably a fourth of it. I never claimed we were a classy bunch.

We waddled out of the sidewalk café and down the streets of Quebec. Still, we had a little time left before we had to meet the others at the bus for our tour of Old Quebec City. As he sat in the grass on the grounds of the old Parliament building waiting for the bus, Sam decided to call the kennel back home and see how the dog was getting along. The kennel master assured him that she was eating well and playing nicely with the other dogs so he decided to treat her to a shampoo, haircut, and a manicure. Okay, he had her nails trimmed. Spoiled? No, I don't think so, do you? The bus arrived almost on time and we boarded quickly because we were ready to see all the sights.

The bus stopped at a scenic overlook supposedly to see a statue of one of Quebec's forefathers. We all filed off the bus with our cameras in hand. When we neared the large statue, we found what looked like a smaller statue made of alabaster. It was the whitest white you have ever seen. In fact, the face, bald head, ears, neck, and hands were all totally white and everything else was draped in white. Then we noticed the sunglasses and … duh! It was not a statue but a college student posing as a statue. His arms were outstretched but if someone put coins in his urn, he would change his stance by folding his hands in a prayer-like position. He was good. I think it was the sunglasses that gave him away though. Really? Yeah, I'm pretty sure.

After driving around the walled city of Old Quebec and seeing buildings and architecture that dated back to the 15th century (I think), we were able to get off the bus and go on a walking tour. The city is built on hills, really high hills. The Frontenac Hotel was the grandest building on the highest hill. Personally, we never made it to the Frontenac but I understand that some did. There was a cable car to take you up and bring you back down. It was $2.50 to go up and $2.50 to come back down but it would have taken more time than we wanted to spend. Really, it wasn't the money.

This same area was the locality where the scene from *Catch Me If You Can* was filmed where Leonardo di Caprio was finally caught. We went into the church that was a part of that final scene. Outside in the square, there were street performers standing along the brick streets entertaining the vacationers and shoppers. We enjoyed the talents of an opera singer standing by the curb singing her arias with nothing but her boom box to accompany her. There was a flutist, music stand in front of her, playing music that could have come straight from the forest. There was a folk singer that made me think I was back in the 60s, and a violinist who could have kept Ireland free from snakes … or was it rats? On another corner was a man who made music using partially filled water goblets. Years ago when we made that noise in restaurants, we only did it to annoy people. But when he made that noise, it was the most beautiful music I have ever heard. My only regret is that I didn't buy one of his tapes. There was so much to see. We shopped in the stores, watched people, and enjoyed seeing the biggest mural I have ever seen painted on the side of a building. The mural depicted some of the history of Old Quebec and even though we knew it was a mural, one would swear there really were balconies and porches, stairways and windows, people and animals, and more. I would like to go back there too.

After touring on foot, I think most of us looked forward to getting back on the bus just so we could sit down. It had been quite a day and we had a long way to go before we slept that night. Supper was scheduled for 6:15 in Montreal and after supper, more bus riding to our next stop, our motel.

We stopped for dinner at a neat little Italian "all you can eat" restaurant and after that we were on our way again. Like always, we were running late but that night no one minded because we were seeing Montreal by the artificial city lights that are hauntingly beautiful. It was a clear night and you see things at night you wouldn't notice during the day. We still had a long way to go before we got to our motel but with any kind of luck we would have been sawing logs by 11:00. That's still pretty late when you figure we had to have our luggage ready for pickup by 7:45 the next morning. Oh well.

Darkness had fallen and the night was almost black once we left the bright lights of Montreal. We were traveling right along at a steady pace while some of us slept, some were reading, a few were engaged in conversation when all at once we pulled off the road and stopped on the berm. We were in the middle of nowhere and everyone became eerily quiet—waiting for an explanation. Kurt, our driver, informed us that the other bus had a flat tire. He got out and went to see how bad the problem was. It was about 9:15 and had started to rain.

Maybe it was the dark night, maybe it was the rain, but the roads in Canada seemed much narrower than roads in the United States. Possibly it was just that Canadian roads don't have much shoulder room. Or perhaps, we were getting a little apprehensive. We were off the side of the road as far as we could go safely but every time a car or truck would pass by, the bus shook. You know that suction you feel when you're standing too close to fast moving traffic? That's what it was like. Kind of scary—it felt like something could take us out at any time but everyone remained calm. Kurt and Schultz decided that the best thing to do was for Kurt to take us and find a place where we could wait in safety while he returned for the passengers on the injured bus. He would then bring them to where we waited while the bus was being repaired. The disabled bus could not be moved. There had been a major blowout and the tire was off the rim and the bus couldn't be driven.

Kurt came back to our bus and announced the plan. We wasted no time. Leaving the others by the side of the road, we went in search of a safe place to wait. We came to a wide spot in the road where there was a restaurant/bar. From the outside, it appeared too small to accommodate all of us but Kurt stopped to see if there was anything larger nearby. That proved to be a good move as we were able to get directions to an all-night McDonald's just a couple miles away. It took quite a while to get directions because Kurt didn't speak French and the people giving directions spoke very little English.

It was about 10:15 p.m. when we arrived at McDonald's. Kurt checked with the people on duty there and they welcomed us warmly and gave their permission for us to wait there as long as we needed. At least that's what it sounded like they were saying. They didn't speak English but they were very gracious as we descended on their restaurant like it was a flea market in Florida and just sort of plunked our old bodies down in an out-of-the-way area. Kurt wasted no time in getting back on the bus and retracing his steps to pick up the others that were waiting in the disabled bus by the side of the road. They were very brave.

At the restaurant, we were just plain McMuddled! As usual, we ate like pigs at the buffet earlier in the evening so no one was hungry. A few ordered coffee or hot chocolate but that was about it. McDonald's wasn't going to make any money on this group. Before long, decks of cards appeared. There were two couples next to us who began playing bridge. We looked through all of our belongings to see if anyone had a deck of cards so that we could play Euchre. When we came up empty, the bridge players graciously offered their second deck so that we could pass the time a little more pleasantly too.

Did I mention that Garry and Cookie are our best friends? Well, after three games of cutthroat Euchre with Garry, I ain't never playin' Euchre with him again. Yes, he and Cookie won, but that has nothing to do with my decision to only play with civilized people. Maybe if he promised to be more pleasant—maybe.

At 11:00 or so, Kurt arrived with the passengers from the other bus. They seemed relieved to be out of the disabled bus and off the side of the road. Gretchen, their escort, charged in like she owned the place and brought with her a walloping big box of donuts that she had bought somewhere else. Now wouldn't you think that if the good people at McDonald's were willing to let us sit at their tables, use their bathrooms, and play cards in their dining room without buying anything, we should eat only food purchased there if we eat anything at all? It seemed to me that bringing food into McDonald's was insulting to those gracious people who were so hospitable to us. Back to my story. After passing out the donuts, Gretchen yelled for everybody to be quiet. (I thought I heard a "shut up" but I'm not positive on that.) All card playing had to be toned down because Gretchen had spoken. The next words out of her mouth were, "N-36, B-9, 0-75, etc." Her BINGO game took over the entire area.

Meanwhile, Kurt and Schultz went to work on the side of the road repairing the tire. One of them—probably Schultz—called the home office of the tour Bus Company and they sent someone to get the tire back on the rim. The scuttlebutt at McDonald's was that Kurt was working in his shirtsleeves under the bus in the rain. He truly was the real hero of our trip. Finally, at about twenty minutes to one, he had the tire back on the bus and the bus was on its way back to McDonald's, the Bingo stopped, and re-boarding began.

After everyone had gotten back on the proper bus and the busses pulled out of the lot, we were still an hour away from our motel and a half a night's sleep. Then it started again. The lights on bus #1 started flashing and we pulled off the road once more. Schultz couldn't steer the bus. Something was wrong. At this point, Kurt got out and crawled under the bus and saw that there was tire rubber wound around some kind of rod. It was raining. He worked until he got the rubber unwound and while he was doing all of that, I fell asleep. When I woke up, we were at the motel in Montreal. It was after 2:00 a.m. and there were no luggage handlers on duty. Sam's medication was in his large suitcase. Don't you think medications really should be kept in one's carry-on? I tried to discuss that with Sam but he wasn't listening. He really needed to get the bags from under the bus but he had to carry them himself. Kurt offered to carry luggage but no one had the gall to ask him to do anything but sleep the rest of that night. By the time I brushed my teeth and turned in, it was 3:15 a.m. We left a wake up call for 6:45 so we would be up, showered, dressed, and have our luggage outside our door and be ready for breakfast by 8:00. I wish we had known we weren't leaving until 10:30 or later. Some knew, but we didn't.

# Chapter 8

## *Day 7—What Next?*

The next morning we felt about as well rested as parents of small children on Christmas morning. Our departure was delayed from 8:00 to 10:30 in order that the bus drivers could sleep. Not everyone was aware of the change, however, until the next morning at breakfast. All we really wanted to do was go home and see the dog. But no—Toronto beckoned. At this moment, our Canadian Castle Tour seemed to be one big potty break/meal stop/problem. What else could possibly go wrong?

The bus got rolling about 10:45. We were on our way to Toronto and the CN Tower. At approximately 11:00, a car pulled right in front of our bus and Kurt slammed on the breaks in order to avoid a collision. Phyllis was thrown into the front windshield and Jesse was at her side in no time checking to see if she were okay and helping her to get up. Mona, a lady sitting about three fourths of the way back on the right hand side was bleeding from a cut on her ankle. She had been trying to get comfortable by sitting across two seats with her feet elevated because her ankles were so swollen from too much sitting the day before. Standing halfway in the isle behind Mona helping her put a pillow behind her back, was Charlotte, another passenger. When the bus slammed to an abrupt halt, Charlotte was thrown forward and fell into the aisle. When she fell, somehow, something cut into Mona's ankle and caused a wound that wouldn't stop bleeding. It wasn't life threatening. It was just that Mona was on aspirin therapy and her blood was very thin and wouldn't clot easily. There were a couple of medical people amongst our ranks, Vickie and Marge, and they pitched in immediately, tending to the wounded until help arrived. Kurt pulled the bus to the curb in order to assess the injuries and to see if anyone needed to be taken to the hospital.

In the meantime, Schultz witnessed the accident and when the driver of the aforementioned car stopped at a traffic light, she told him that he had caused an accident that had produced injuries and he needed to stop. He said he would but when the light changed, he took off. Schultz took off after him. I can just see that in my mind's eye—a big tour bus full of senior citizens chasing a little red car. Wouldn't that be a sight? Picture it. A bus full of senior citizens tearing down city streets and back alleys, cornering that bus on two, no, four, no, eight wheels, chasing a perp in a get-a-way car. She overtakes him and pulls the bus right in front of his car and he has to stop. She leaps off the bus, handcuffs in hand, and makes a citizen's arrest. It paints a mental picture, doesn't it? Well, that **didn't** happen.

Needless to say, she lost him in traffic but did manage to

keep up for a couple of blocks. They gave up the chase and headed back to our bus to see if we needed help. The observant people on the other bus were able to get the license number, car make and model, description, etc. Meanwhile, back at our bus, Kurt called 911 and before anyone could say "Houston, we have a problem." an ambulance arrived. First on the scene were the EMTs. They boarded the bus and checked passengers for injuries. The police got there soon after and tried to listen to thirty people talking at once, everyone trying to tell them what had happened. The Canadian police were very polite but they didn't speak much English. Kurt was required to file a report because people were injured. Because of the aspirin therapy, it took Mona a while to stop bleeding but she was not seriously hurt. Do you think the Canadian police ever went after that guy? I wonder.

That delay set us back, timewise. Undaunted though, we were under way once more. This time, lunch was on our own and when we stopped, we were allowed 45 minutes to get fast food and bring it back to the bus to eat it on the way to supper.

We were too far behind schedule to keep our reservations to see the CN Tower in Toronto, Ontario. Instead, the plans were changed to include a stop at 1000 Islands Observation Point and Gift Shop. In my opinion, everyone enjoyed the change of plans. Instead of climbing, we took the elevator to the top of the observation tower overlooking the 1000 Islands of the St. Lawrence River, most of which had private homes built on them. There was even a castle built on one island. We didn't see that one but there was a picture of it on the wall in the tower. The gift shop there was one of the nicest we had seen and I couldn't resist buying a ceramic eagle that was made in Canada by Canadians.

Supper that night was at the *Town & Country* buffet in Toronto. Some liked it. Some hated it. Personally, I was getting tired of eating out and I think I would have traded my right arm for some homemade chicken noodle soup and a half a grilled cheese sandwich made on homemade bread. I have no idea what we ate that night. We didn't go hungry.

When we had finished eating, it was only a short ride to the hotel in Mississauga, Ontario. We needed our entire luggage collection and, once again, we were on the second floor and there was no elevator. By then, I just wanted to go home. I missed the dog. We managed.

# Chapter 9

## *Day 8—The Edsel Ford Mansion*

Bon jour! We awoke this morning wondering what day it was and where we were. Ye gods, we were still in Canada! Another day had begun with another continental breakfast—bagels and coffee, something new to look forward to. Maybe not. As we were waiting for the waitress to bring our complimentary bowl of cereal and slice of toast, (no bagels) I struck up a conversation with the woman next to me who happened to be from the other bus. As we were discussing the happenings of the last few days, Gretchen approached the table, interrupting us as she neared, and began to scold my new acquaintance for expressing her opinion of their leadership. She said her piece, turned, and left.

"What was that all about?" I said.

"She's been upset the whole trip about one thing or another," my companion said. "I just don't pay any attention to her." And we continued on with our conversation.

When we finished breakfast, we stopped at the front desk

to tell them about our toilet that was stopped up. It wouldn't flush. That was our biggest problem so far that day. It was early though; there was still time.

We were only fifteen minutes late leaving. The day showed promise; we were headed toward home.

But first, we had one last tour. This time we were headed to the Edsel and Eleanor Ford Home in Grosse Pointe, Michigan. But before we got to the Ford Home, we stopped at the Duty Free Shop on the Canadian side of the St. Lawrence River. Liz needed to get rid of the wine she had purchased the night before. She had her little bottle and was drinking wine from a plain brown paper bag. Of course, she wasn't a wino but the brown bag thing was something to see. Before we crossed the border, we needed to get rid of any remaining Canadian money. Also, we had time to shop and use the facilities. As we entered the Duty Free Store, everyone headed for the bathroom so I decided to shop first. After about 15 minutes I returned to the restroom area only to be told by Schultz who was waiting on the other side of the turnstile that I couldn't go back through. (Actually, I was going to use the gate beside the turnstile) She said I must go all the way through the store, out the exit, walk around the outside of the building and re-enter the store in order to get to the restroom that was ten feet away. I declined. I said I would do that the next time, but for now—I was going to the bathroom and I opened the gate and went through it. Shopping was fun at the Duty Free Store. They had great prices on liquor and chocolate, perfume, and cigarettes. We were advised to pay with a credit card because the exchange rate was much better that way. The lower prices were reflected on our credit card bill. It showed the higher Canadian prices and the amount that we actually paid which was considerably less.

At last, it was time to reenter the United States. Once the Canadian Security Guard had boarded and checked us out, we were free to cross the border. We passed through customs without incident. Finally, we were back in the good old U. S. of A. First stop—McDonald's because lunch was on our own. McDonald's on the American side seemed so much homier after being away. We got our lunch and returned to the bus so we could get going. Oops! Liz spilled her coffee on the floor and it all headed for the front of the bus—on both sides. This is the same woman who was drinking the contents of her open wine bottle from a brown paper bag before she got to customs. Coincidence? Could be. Martha fell in the parking lot at McDonald's and skinned her elbow. She's okay.

Just for the record, she didn't have a thing to drink. It's just that old people fall down occasionally.

We were only ½ hour late for our next stop, the Eleanor and Edsel Ford mansion. This was a good stop. I was sure that I wouldn't like it because I just wanted to keep going so we would be home sooner. Since I couldn't change it, I made the best of it.

Staff members at the mansion graciously welcomed us. They split us up into smaller groups and assigned a guide to each group. The guides seemed to be exceptionally knowledgeable about the Ford family, the home, and the famous guests who had frequented it. Even though we wanted to go home, we couldn't help but be brought into the moment as we went from room to room in this grand estate. What struck me most was the fact that the home and grounds were all set up with family in mind. Our tour ended with a trip through a playhouse that had been a gift to the Ford children from a visiting dignitary. It was made of brick, had a kitchen, living room, bedroom, bathroom, and playroom and cost $15,000 in 1935. It was hardly ever played in.

But then it was back to reality and the bus. We were on the road again running a good hour and a half behind schedule. Jesse popped another movie into the VCR and we were makin' time. The movie was a Sylvester Stallone, John Lithgow film called *Cliffhanger*. I didn't care for it at all. Or should I say, "I don't give a f___ for that s___." The language was that bad. Please excuse me, but I was trying to make a point.

While we were riding along watching the movie we had a close call with a burning car. It happened so fast. One minute we were cruising along just fine and the next, Kurt hit the brakes and yelled, "hold on." Just that fast, we were driving through thick smoke and we couldn't see a thing. There we were, traveling at highway speeds and you couldn't see your hand in front of your face. It seemed like we were in smoke forever but it was only a few seconds and then it was gone. Thank God, no one was hurt. We had been through so much already that a car fire (ho hum) didn't command much attention.

Bob Evans Restaurant was our destination for supper. It was late when we arrived and we were not served right away. By the time everyone had been served and had eaten and gotten back on the bus it was almost 9:00. Still, we had about a 2-hour journey to the motel. Nothing more held us up and we arrived safely and were in our rooms by 11:00. It was time to relax because tomorrow we were headed for home. Our departure time was extended a little the next day so we could, for the first time, sleep in.

# Chapter 10

## *Day 9—Home Sweet Home*

The final day of our trip and all I can say is "yippy skippy and hip hip hooray!" We're goin' home. We wondered why we ever wanted to leave home in the first place. Let's call the kids. Whatever did we do before cell phones? Sam retired because he didn't want to deal with computers and the new age of technology. Now he e-mails his old cronies, writes letters on a word processor, and calls the dog from Canada on a cell phone.

Ah, the cell phone. It was time to call the kids. First he called his daughter on her cell phone. She told him that while we were gone, the horn alarm sounded on our car in the middle of the night. Our car was in a locked garage with both garage door openers tucked safely inside. Eventually it stopped but not before there were several phone calls made to several people. Most of our neighbors were still speaking to us when we got home.

We woke up early that final day and ate breakfast in our room, just the two of us. Our trip was almost over and we couldn't believe all that had happened in such a short time. Everyone was ready to get back on the bus. Everyone except the disabled woman and her husband. They made a grand entrance as the final couple to board the bus. Kurt was ready to ease out of the parking space as soon as they were seated. He no sooner began to back up than she got out of her seat and headed for the bathroom. That would be a very difficult thing for her to do when the bus was stopped but impossible when the bus was in motion. Kurt stopped the bus and waited for her to complete her trek up the aisle and back before he continued toward home. I overheard her say, "I had to go before we got on the bus but my husband said, 'No, we have to go.'" Taking a few minutes extra would have been so much easier for her.

Now only one more stop before home. Burger King, but this was the last stop, the last "lunch on our own." After that was Whitewater. For the first time on this trip, we were ahead of schedule. There were those who hated to see it end but I think the majority were ready to resume their normal lives.

With the Whitewater group delivered all safe and sound, we were on the final leg of our trip to Fort Atkinson. We were so happy to be going home. Chad had left a car for the four of us in the parking lot. We didn't have to wait for a ride. It wouldn't be long now.

We pulled into the K-Mart Parking lot, said our good-byes, and headed for the car. Our luggage barely fit but we were only a minute and a half from home so we held some of it on our laps. No problem.

Garry and Cookie dropped us off at our house and they

were on their way. This sounds like the end, right? Wrong! We didn't have a key to get in. Both of our cars were locked securely in the garage with the garage door openers clamped safely to the visors. We had not hidden a key outside. After all, we had just moved in. Our luggage and we were locked out of our house and I really wanted to get in so I could use my brand new bathroom. What did we do? Just what we would do if we got a new computer, we asked our granddaughter for help. Grandchildren to the rescue! When we called, our granddaughter was breast feeding our great granddaughter. She dropped everything, (not literally) got a key and hurried over. At last, we were in our house. The door leading into the garage was off its hinges because it needed to be cut off to fit over the new kitchen floor. That's okay; we'll get to it. The bathroom was nowhere near finished. In fact, there wasn't even a toilet. Fortunately, there was one in the basement. Ahhhh. It's good to be home.

Would we do it again? You betcha! But not for a long time and only with one bus. And next time I would take along a palm pilot, lap desk, extra hand sanitizer wipes, Rolaids, crosswords, and MRE's (Meals Ready to Eat, Army combat food) to combat the fast food. As for tonight, supper is on our own!

# The End